The Easter Cub

By Justine Korman Fontes
Illustrated by Lucinda McQueen

Hello Reader! — Level 2

SCHOLASTIC INC. Cartwheel ·B·O·O·K·S·®
New York   Toronto   London   Auckland   Sydney
Mexico City   New Delhi   Hong Kong   Buenos Aires

Hello, Family Members,

Learning to read is one of the most important accomplishments of early childhood. **Hello Reader!** books are designed to help children become skilled readers who like to read. Beginning readers learn to read by remembering frequently used words like "the," "is," and "and"; by using phonics skills to decode new words; and by interpreting picture and text clues. These books provide both the stories children enjoy and the structure they need to read fluently and independently. Here are suggestions for helping your child *before*, *during*, and *after* reading:

Before
- Look at the cover and pictures and have your child predict what the story is about.
- Read the story to your child.
- Encourage your child to chime in with familiar words and phrases.
- Echo read with your child by reading a line first and having your child read it after you do.

During
- Have your child think about a word he or she does not recognize right away. Provide hints such as "Let's see if we know the sounds" and "Have we read other words like this one?"
- Encourage your child to use phonics skills to sound out new words.
- Provide the word for your child when more assistance is needed so that he or she does not struggle and the experience of reading with you is a positive one.
- Encourage your child to have fun by reading with a lot of expression . . . like an actor!

After
- Have your child keep lists of interesting and favorite words.
- Encourage your child to read the books over and over again. Have him or her read to brothers, sisters, grandparents, and even teddy bears. Repeated readings develop confidence in young readers.
- Talk about the stories. Ask and answer questions. Share ideas about the funniest and most interesting characters and events in the stories.

I do hope that you and your child enjoy this book.

—Francie Alexander
   Chief Education Officer,
   Scholastic Education

For Dr. Skip—

May there always be a smile beneath your mustache!

−J.K.F.

For Edie—

Many, many thanks!

−L.M.

Text copyright © 2003 by Justine Korman Fontes.
Illustrations copyright © 2003 by Lucinda McQueen.
All rights reserved. Published by Scholastic Inc.
SCHOLASTIC, HELLO READER, CARTWHEEL BOOKS, and associated logos
are trademarks and/or registered trademarks of Scholastic Inc.

Library of Congress Cataloging-in-Publication Data

Korman Fontes, Justine.
   The Easter cub / by Justine Korman Fontes ; illustrated by Lucinda McQueen.
      p. cm. — (Hello Reader! Level 2)
Summary: Pip the curious cub notices that signs of spring are appearing around him, finds out more about the season from Evergreen the tree, and joins the children in the cabin as they celebrate Easter.
   ISBN 0-439-44340-7 (alk. paper)
   [1. Spring — Fiction. 2. Easter — Fiction. 3. Bears — Fiction.
4. Trees — Fiction.] I. McQueen, Lucinda, ill. II. Title. III. Series.
PZ7.K83692 Eas 2003
[E] — dc21   2002007728

10 9 8 7 6 5 4 3   03 04 05 06 07
            Printed in the U.S.A. 23 • First printing, February 2003

Once there was a
curious cub named Pip.
Everything was new to him!
One morning, Pip felt the snow melt
under his paws.
Why is it so soft and wet? Pip wondered.
"It's spring! It's spring!" the birds chirped.
Pip was surprised.
The birds had been quiet for so long.
Why were they suddenly chirping again?
And what was spring? He wanted to know.

Pip heard a stream splashing.
The stream had been frozen solid
and was silent all winter.
Now the stream babbled,
"It's spring! It's spring!"

Pip wondered, *What is spring?*
Suddenly, a flock of geese filled the sky
over Pip's head.
"It's spring! It's spring!"
the geese honked.
Pip exclaimed, "I must find out
what spring is!"

So he decided to visit his friend Evergreen.
The wise tree had lived for many years
near a cozy cabin.
Evergreen knew all kinds of things.
She had told Pip all about winter
and Christmas.
Evergreen was sure to know
about spring, too.

And she did! Evergreen told Pip all about spring.

From then on, Pip looked for new signs
of spring every day.
Suddenly, the trees weren't bare anymore.
Pip saw tight, little green buds
on the branches!
Then he saw purple petals
pushing through the soft snow.

He ran to tell Evergreen the exciting news!
Evergreen laughed.
"You found crocuses.
But you haven't seen anything yet!
The purple ones are just some of the
first flowers in spring.
Spring gets even better."

Evergreen was right.

In the warm days that followed,

Pip found more and more flowers!

Each kind was pretty in its own special way.

"Now I know all about spring,"
Pip told Evergreen.
"And it's wonderful!"
But the tree shook her branches.
"Spring gets even better."
And it was true!

Soon Pip was surprised by even
more signs of spring.
The tight green buds opened into
fresh new leaves!
Bright green grass pushed its way
through the soft ground.
Grasshoppers hopped!
Clover bloomed!
And bees flew by buzzing,
"It's spring! It's spring!"

"Now I really know all about spring!" Pip told Evergreen. But the tree chuckled. "Wait! Spring gets even better!"

One day, Pip peeked in the windows
of the cozy cabin.
The people were painting colors on eggs.
"Why are they doing that?"
Pip asked Evergreen.
"Because tomorrow is Easter,"
the wise tree said.
Pip asked, "What is *Easter*?"

"Easter is a holiday that celebrates
all the new things that spring brings,"
Evergreen explained.
Then she told Pip about the Easter Bunny
and how the bunny hides treats for children.
"That sounds like fun!" Pip cried.
"I wish I were the Easter Bunny!
I wish I had treats to hide and give!"

Evergreen sighed.
"You should be happy
being what you are.
A cute and curious cub
is quite special enough."

Pip still wished he could do things
like the Easter Bunny.

But the next morning was such a beautiful
Easter morning that Pip felt happy —
even if he was *just a bear.*
His mother kissed him and said,
"Good morning! I love you."
Pip kissed her back and said,
"Happy Easter! I love you, too."
Right then, Pip knew that he did have
something to give: His love!

So on the way to visit Evergreen,
Pip stopped to kiss everything he loved
and to wish them all a Happy Easter.
He kissed the daffodils... and they
tickled his nose.

Pip kissed the clover... and it tickled his toes.

He kissed the pussywillows
and the new green leaves.
Pip was having a great time!

But he had the funny feeling
he was being watched. . . .

Pip turned around quickly.

And he saw the Easter Bunny!

"I've been watching you spread Easter joy,"
the Bunny said.

"You're doing a good job, for a bear!"

"Would you like to hide some treats
for the children who live in the cabin?"
the Easter Bunny asked.
"Oh, yes!" Pip squeaked. "Thanks!"

Pip had a great time hiding treats!

He had even more fun watching the children
look for the treats.
Pip hid behind Evergreen's branches
and listened to the children's squeals of joy.
He felt all warm and giggly.

Pip whispered to Evergreen,
"Does spring get any better than this?"
Evergreen shook her shiny needles.
"No," she said, sighing.
"This is spring at its best."

Pip sighed, too.
Then he kissed his green friend
and said, "I love you, Evergreen.
Happy Easter!"